P9-CBS-257

The Primary Source Library of the Thirteen Colonies and the Lost Colony ™

The Colony of Pennsylvania

A Primary Source History

The Rosen Publishing Group's
PowerKids Press ™
PRIMARY SOURCE

Melody S. Mis

To Judith and Gary Thomas, who would rather be in New York

Published in 2007 by The Rosen Publishing Group, Inc.
29 East 21st Street, New York, NY 10010

Copyright © 2007 by The Rosen Publishing Group, Inc.

All rights reserved. No part of this book may be reproduced in any form without permission in writing from the publisher, except by a reviewer.

First Edition

Editor: Jennifer Way
Book Design: Ginny Chu
Layout Design: Julio A. Gil
Photo Researcher: Gabriel Caplan

Photo Credits: Cover and title page Private Collection/ © John Noott Galleries, Broadway, Worcestershire, UK/ The Bridgeman Art Library; p. 4 Library of Congress Geography and Map Division; p. 4 (inset) Government of Ontario Art Collection, 619849; pp. 6 (left), 12 (left) Pennsylvania Historical and Museum Commission, Pennsylvania State Archives; pp. 6 (right), 8 (left) © Atwater Kent Museum of Philadelphia, Courtesy of the Historical Society of Pennsylvania / Bridgeman Art Library; p. 8 (right) The Historical Society of Pennsylvania, Society Collection (Of 610/1683); p. 10 (left) American Philosophical Society; pp. 10 (right), 18 (left) Private Collection/ Bridgeman Art Library; pp. 12 (right), 16 (left) The Philadelphia Museum of Art/ Art Resource, NY; p. 14 (left) Library of Congress; p. 14 (right) The National Archives of the UK (PRO): ref. MR 1/518; p. 16 (right) The New York Public Library/Art Resource, NY; p. 18 (right) © The National Archives/HIP/The Image Works; p. 20 (left) U.S. National Archives and Records Administration; p. 20 (right) © The Image Works Archives.

Library of Congress Cataloging-in-Publication Data

Mis, Melody S.
    The colony of Pennsylvania : a primary source history / Melody S. Mis.— 1st ed.
        p. cm. — (The primary source library of the thirteen colonies and the Lost Colony)
    Includes index.
    ISBN 1-4042-3437-3 (library binding)
    1. Pennsylvania—History—Colonial period, ca. 1600–1775—Juvenile literature. 2. Pennsylvania—History—1775–1865—Juvenile literature. 3. Pennsylvania—History—Colonial period, ca. 1600–1775—Sources-Juvenile literature. 4. Pennsylvania—History—1775–1865—Sources—Juvenile literature. I. Title. II. Series.
    F152.M6 2007
    974.8'02—dc22
                            2005027865

Manufactured in the United States of America

Contents

Susquehanna River

This is a close-up view of a Dutch map of the East Coast of North America from around 1639.
It shows the land that would become Pennsylvania. Étienne Brulé traveled down the
Susquehanna River, which has been shaded blue. Inset: Brulé is believed to have been the first
European to see Pennsylvania. Here he is shown meeting with Native Americans.

Discovering Pennsylvania

Native American people began living in Pennsylvania about 10,000 years ago. The Lenni-Lenape lived in eastern Pennsylvania along the Delaware River. The Susquehannock lived in central Pennsylvania. The Monongahela, Shawnee, and Erie lived in western Pennsylvania.

Some historians believe that the first European to see Pennsylvania was a Frenchman named Étienne Brulé. In 1615, Brulé traveled down the Susquehanna River through Pennsylvania. France wanted to trade with the Native Americans for furs. These furs would then be sold to Europeans to make coats and hats. In 1643, Swedish settlers founded the first colony in Pennsylvania. They called their settlement New Sweden. In 1655, Dutch soldiers from New York seized New Sweden. They held it until 1664, when England took over.

From the Charter of Pennsylvania

"Wee have hereby made and ordained the aforesaid William Penn, his heires and assignee, the true and absolute Proprietaries of all the Lands and Dominions aforesaid, KNOW YE THEREFORE, That We reposing speciall trust and Confidence in the fidelitie, wisedom, Justice, and provident circumspection of the said William Penn . . . Doe grant free, full, and absolute power and vertue of these presents to him and his heires."

This part of Pennsylvania's charter says that Charles II trusts William Penn. He then gives Penn, his family, and the people he appoints control of the Pennsylvania colony.

Sir William Penn lived from 1621 until 1670. He served in England's navy and won battles and took land for the English Crown. To honor the Penn family's service to their country, Charles II gave Penn's son William land in North America. Inset: Charles II gave William Penn a charter for Pennsylvania in 1681.

William Penn's Experiment

In 1681, Charles II, king of England, gave William Penn land in North America. Charles II named the land Pennsylvania, which means "Penn's Woods." Penn planned to establish a colony there for **Quakers** and other groups that were being **persecuted** in England. Penn called his plan the **Holy** Experiment.

Penn led a group of Quakers to Pennsylvania in August 1682. They called their settlement Philadelphia. Penn bought land from the Lenni-Lenape. He told them he wanted to live in peace. Penn also promised the Swedes living in Pennsylvania that they would be ruled fairly under his plan, the First Frame of Government.

The Quakers are also known as the Society of Friends, which is their official name. The group was founded in England in the 1640s. They were nicknamed "Quakers," because they said that people should quake, or tremble, in the presence of God.

The Quakers were persecuted because they refused to go to war. Many were jailed, and others had their property taken away from them.

In 1681, William Markham created a layout for the city of Philadelphia before colonists even moved there. After they arrived Penn and the colonists built homes along the wide streets. Inset: In 1682, William Penn signed a treaty, or agreement, with the Lenni-Lenape, Susquehannock, and Shawnee.

Settling Philadelphia

In 1681, William Penn sent the colony's first governor, William Markham, to lay out the town of Philadelphia. It was the first planned city in the British colonies. Penn's plan for Philadelphia included wide streets and public parks.

Penn and his group arrived in October 1682. They built homes along the town's streets and planted gardens. Some of the newcomers learned how to build log cabins from the Swedish settlers.

Penn also held a meeting in 1682, with the Lenni-Lenape, Susquehannock, and Shawnee. They signed the Great Treaty. It said that the Native Americans and settlers would live in peace. Chief Tamanend of the Lenni-Lenape gave Penn a friendship belt. It showed a Quaker and a Native American shaking hands. The chief gave Penn the belt to honor the event.

From the Charter of Privileges

"I do hereby grant and declare, That no Person or Persons, inhabiting in this Province or Territories. . . shall be in any Case molested or prejudiced . . . because of his or their conscientious Persuasion or Practice, nor be compelled to frequent or maintain any religious Worship, Place or Ministry, contrary to his or their Mind, or to do or super any other Act or Thing, contrary to their religious Persuasion."

This part of the Charter of Privileges says that people who live in the colony have the right to worship as they choose. It also says that the government cannot demand that people do something that is against their beliefs.

When Penn was in his early twenties, he joined the Quaker religion. He was jailed several times for writing and speaking about his religious beliefs. When Penn established Pennsylvania, the colony allowed people to practice their religion freely. Inset: William Penn wrote the Charter of Privileges in 1701.

Pennsylvania's Early Years

Between 1682 and 1700, Pennsylvania's population grew from about 500 to 18,000. Several towns were established, including Lancaster. Lancaster was founded by Germans. Although there were a few slaves in Pennsylvania, Quakers and many other settlers did not agree with slavery. In 1688, Germantown passed the British colonies' first law banning slavery.

In 1684, William Penn sailed to England, where he remained for 15 years. In 1701, he wrote the **Charter** of **Privileges**. The charter made Pennsylvania the first American colony to have a **democratic** government. It gave the colonists more power in making laws. It also **guaranteed** their **civil rights**. It remained Pennsylvania's form of government until 1776. After the Charter of Privileges was completed, Penn returned to England. He would never return to Pennsylvania.

Benjamin Franklin was an inventor and a scientist. Franklin was born in Boston, Massachusetts, in 1706. In 1723, Franklin moved to Philadelphia, where he started his own newspaper, called the Pennsylvania Gazette. Inset: The Walking Purchase of 1737 cheated the Lenni-Lenape out of a lot of their land. William Penn's sons Thomas and John were among the men who drew up this document.

Colonial Pennsylvania

Between 1700 and 1750, Pennsylvania grew from 18,000 to 120,000 people. Philadelphia was the colony's capital. Pennsylvania's **assembly** met in the State House, which is now known as Independence Hall. Philadelphia was also the home of Benjamin Franklin. Franklin established America's first library. He also founded a school that would become the University of Pennsylvania.

Pennsylvania was becoming a successful colony. However, its leaders failed to keep their promises to the Lenni-Lenape. While William Penn had been in charge, the colonists had treated the local Native Americans fairly. After Penn left in 1701, many colonists began to cheat them out of their land. The colonists' actions came to be called the Walking Purchase of 1737. The Walking Purchase hurt relations between the Lenni-Lenape and the colonists.

JOIN, or DIE.

Fort Pitt, near today's Pittsburgh, was the location of several important battles in the French and Indian War. The British finally won the fort from the French in 1758. Inset: Ben Franklin drew and printed this cartoon in his newspaper, the Pennsylvania Gazette, in 1754. The cartoon shows that the colonies should join together to fight the French and Indian War.

Great Britain Taxes the Colonies

Beginning in 1754, Britain fought the French and Indian War over the control of North America. A major battle of the war was fought in Pennsylvania at Fort Pitt. Britain won the war in 1763, but had run up a large **debt**. To pay this debt, Britain taxed the colonies.

The colonists hated these taxes. They were also angry because they were not **represented** in Britain's government. Britain's government decided the colonies' laws and taxes. A tax on paper goods, called the Stamp Act, was passed in 1765. The colonists became angrier. Benjamin Franklin **protested** by printing newspaper stories that suggested that people fight Britain's taxes. Some Pennsylvanians protested the Stamp Act by joining the **Sons of Liberty**. The group often burned the stamps or attacked the stamp collectors. The colonists objected so much that Britain ended the tax in 1766.

The First Continental Congress was held at Carpenters' Hall in Philadelphia. The hall was also at one time home to Benjamin Franklin's library. Inset: Thomas Mifflin represented Pennsylvania at the First Continental Congress. He helped raise Continental army troops. Later he was a general in the army. This caused him to be thrown out of the Quaker church. Here Mifflin is shown with his wife, Sarah.

Pennsylvania Prepares for Revolution

In 1767, Britain passed another tax. This led John Dickinson from Pennsylvania to write articles protesting the taxes. When Britain tried to end Colonial tea **smuggling** in 1773, a group of Pennsylvanians forced a ship carrying British tea from the harbor. Others protested by boycotting, or refusing to buy, British goods.

Unrest over taxes caused Colonial leaders to call for a meeting to talk about their problems with Britain. The meeting was called the First Continental Congress. It was held in Philadelphia in September 1774. Dickinson, Thomas Mifflin, and Joseph Galloway represented Pennsylvania. At that time the colonies did not want to separate from Britain. They wanted Britain to treat the colonies fairly. Congress realized that their appeals might cause Britain to harm the colonies.

As George III continued to pass taxes on the colonies, he became more unpopular with the colonists. Inset: John Dickinson wrote this letter to King George III in 1775. This was one of the final attempts the Second Continental Congress made to peacefully work out their problems with Great Britain.

The Colonies Meet in Philadelphia

In April 1775, the first battle of the **American Revolution** was fought in Lexington, Massachusetts. The next month Colonial leaders called for the Second Continental Congress to be held in Philadelphia. The Congress met so that they could decide how to work together to fight the British. Pennsylvania's John Dickinson wrote a letter to Britain's king, George III. In it he told the king that Britain did not have the right to tax the colonies. The king paid no attention to the Americans. In reply, the Continental Congress told the 13 colonies to raise troops for a Continental army. It was to be led by General George Washington. Congress realized that independence was the only way to end their problems with Britain. This meant war. The colonies would have to work together to win this war.

The Continental army camped at Valley Forge during the winter of 1777–1778. The camp was troubled by a lack of supplies. They had little food and clothing. They also had poor housing. Inset: *Thomas Jefferson wrote the Declaration of Independence. Members of the Second Continental Congress signed it on July 4, 1776.*

Pennsylvania During the Revolution

In 1776, the war entered its second year. In May 1776, the Second Continental Congress met in Philadelphia. Congress asked Ben Franklin to help write the **Declaration of Independence**. He and eight other Pennsylvanians signed the declaration on July 4, 1776.

The war came to Pennsylvania in September 1777, when the British beat the Americans at the Battle of Brandywine. After the battle the British occupied Philadelphia until the next year. In the winter of 1777, General Washington and his troops set up their camp in Valley Forge, Pennsylvania. It was a terrible time for the Continental army. They did not have enough supplies. Friedrich von Steuben, a German soldier, went to Valley Forge that winter to train the troops. His training helped the Americans win the war. The fighting ended with the Battle of Yorktown in Virginia in 1781.

The Second State

The American Revolution officially ended with the Treaty of Paris. The treaty was signed in 1783. During the Revolution the colonies had followed a set of laws called the Articles of Confederation. These laws did not work. They gave the states more power than the central government. This meant that it was impossible for the states to work together as a single country.

In 1787, leaders of the states met in Philadelphia to form a new government. Their meeting was called the **Constitutional** Convention. A convention is a meeting. Pennsylvania's eight representatives to the convention included Gouverneur Morris, James Wilson, and Ben Franklin. Wilson argued in favor of a stronger central government. On December 12, 1787, Pennsylvania became the second state to join the United States.

Glossary

American Revolution (uh-MER-uh-ken reh-vuh-LOO-shun) Battles that soldiers from the American colonies fought against England for freedom from 1775 to 1781.

assembly (uh-SEM-blee) A group of people who meet to advise a government.

charter (CHAR-tur) An official agreement giving someone permission to do something.

civil rights (SIH-vul RYTS) The rights that citizens have.

constitutional (kon-stih-TOO-shuh-nul) Having to do with the basic rules by which a country is governed.

debt (DET) Something owed.

Declaration of Independence (deh-kluh-RAY-shun UV in-duh-PEN-dints) An official announcement signed on July 4, 1776, in which American colonists stated they were free of British rule.

democratic (deh-muh-KRA-tik) Having to do with a government that is run by the people who live under it.

guaranteed (ger-un-TEED) Promised.

holy (HOH-lee) Blessed.

persecuted (PER-sih-kyoot-ed) Attacked because of one's race or beliefs.

privileges (PRIV-lij-ez) Special rights or favors.

protested (PROH-test-ed) Acted out in disagreement of something.

Quakers (KWAY-kurz) People who belong to a faith that believes in equality for all people, strong families and communities, and peace.

represented (reh-prih-ZENT-ed) Stood for or spoken for by others.

smuggling (SMUH-gling) Bringing something into or out of a country to keep from paying taxes.

Sons of Liberty (SUNZ UV LIH-ber-tee) A group of American colonists who protested the British government before the American Revolution.

Index

Primary Sources

Page 4. Map of New Netherland. Pen and ink and watercolor, circa 1639, Joan Vinckeboons, Library of Congress, Washington, D.C. **Page 6.** *Admiral Sir William Penn.* Oil on canvas, seventeenth century, attributed to Sir Peter Lely, Atwater Kent Museum, Philadelphia. **Page 6. Inset.** Charter of Pennsylvania. March 4, 1681, Pennsylvania State Archives, Harrisburg, Pennsylvania. **Page 8.** Plan of Philadelphia. 1681, Thomas Holme, Historical Society of Pennsylvania, Philadelphia. **Page 10. Inset.** *Charter of Privileges for the Province of Pennsylvania.* 1701, American Philosophical Society, Philadelphia. **Page 12.** Portrait of Benjamin Franklin. Oil on canvas, 1762, Mason Chamberlain, Philadelphia Museum of Art, Philadelphia. **Page 12. Inset.** The Walking Purchase of 1737. August 25, 1737, Pennsylvania State Archives, Harrisburg, Pennsylvania. **Page 14.** Fort Pitt. 1761, The National Archives, Richmond, Surrey, United Kingdom. **Page 14. Inset.** *Join or Die.* Political cartoon, May 9, 1754, Benjamin Franklin, Library of Congress, Washington, D.C. **Page 16.** Carpenter's Hall. Wood engraving, eighteenth century, anonymous, New York Public Library, New York. **Page 16. Inset.** *Portrait of Mr. and Mrs. Thomas Mifflin (Sarah Morris).* Oil on ticking, 1773, John Singleton Copley, Philadelphia Museum of Art, Philadelphia. **Page 18.** "Olive Branch" petition to George III. July 8, 1775, The Image Works, The National Archives, Washington, D.C. **Page 18. Inset.** *Portrait of George III in His Coronation Robes.* Oil on canvas, circa 1760, Allan Ramsay. **Page 20. Inset.** *The Declaration of Independence, printed by Hugh Gaine, 1776.* New-York Historical Society, New York.

Web Sites

Due to the changing nature of Internet links, PowerKids Press has developed an online list of Web sites related to the subject of this book. This site is updated regularly. Please use this link to access the list: www.powerkidslinks.com/pstclc/pennsyl/